BY THE SIDE

OF THE ROAD

Jules Feiffer

MICHAEL DI CAPUA BOOKS • HYPERION BOOKS FOR CHILDREN

To Michael Wolff

I was fooling around in the backseat of the car with my little brother, Rudy.

"Behave," said my father, but we kept fooling around.
"Behave, I mean it," said my father.

But if they stick you in the backseat of a car for two hours, what do they expect?

"I want you to behave, do you hear me?" my mother said, which annoyed me because she's on our side when my father's not around.

But when he is, she switches sides.

"If you don't behave," my father said, "I'm gonna pull over right here, and you can wait by the side of the road till we come and get you."

My brother Rudy decided to behave, which let my father notice
that I was the only one in the car not behaving.

So he parked on the shoulder.

"I'll give you one more chance, Richard," he said. "Either you behave or you get out of this car, and you can wait by the side of the road till I come and get you."

Who likes to be pushed around?

"I think I'll wait by the side of the road," I said.
"Your decision," said my father. And he opened the car door.

I got out.

A little nervous, but who cares? I didn't know where I was. I looked around.

Trees and stuff. A creek. A meadow. A fast-food joint no more than a half mile back.
Actually not a bad place to wait if you're gonna wait by the side of the road.

An hour later I was kind of used to it. Two hours later it was where I wanted to live. Better than my house at least, where my mother and father were always telling me what to do.

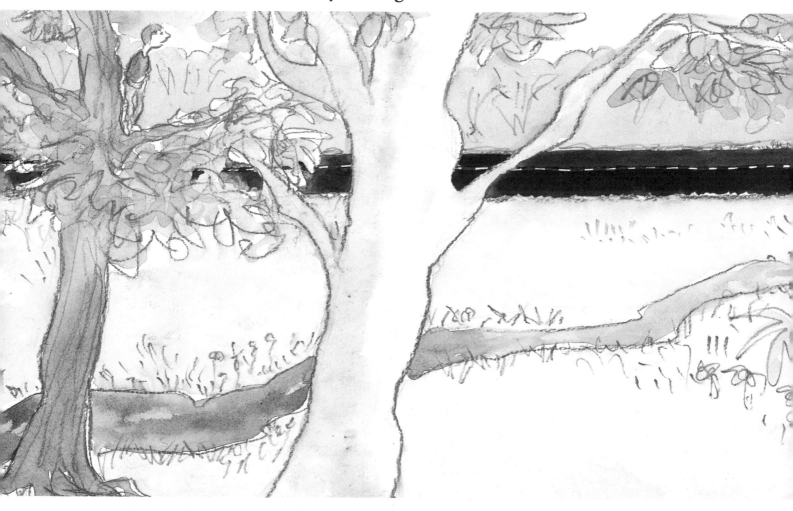

Three hours later when they came back to get me, my father said,
"Have you waited by the side of the road long enough?
I hope you've learned your lesson."

"Not yet," I said. "I think I'd better wait by the side of the road some more."

So he drove off with my mother and my brother Rudy.

I don't know how long before he came back—I was playing kick rocks in the road—
but I know the sun was down behind the fast-food joint.

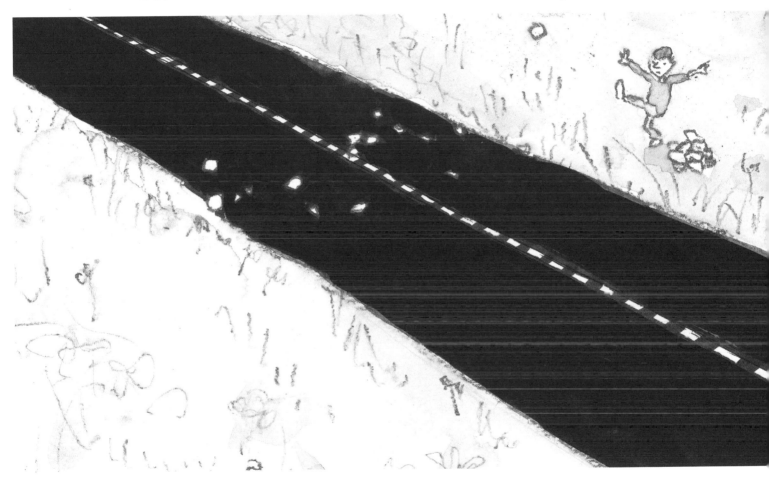

And it had started to get chilly.

And I was thinking: I'm hungry and I'm cold
and I've waited long enough by the side of the road.

At least that's what I was thinking until my father drove up.

He was alone this time. He stuck his head out the window
and called to me, "Learned your lesson yet, wise guy?"

The way he said it made me unlearn the lesson
I was right then in the middle of learning.

So I shook my head and said,
"I better wait a little longer. I could use a hamburger and a sweater, though."

My father drove off to the fast-food joint and came back in a few minutes
with a hamburger and a container of milk.

He knows I hate milk.

Before I could say thank you, because I at least have good manners,
he screeched off, yelling something I couldn't hear.

He came back with my sweater and my mother.
"Please don't do this to me, Richard," she said.

My mother! What was I doing to her?
As far as I could see, the only person being done to was M-E, me!
Right in front of me, there in the dark, my mother and father had a fight

about whose fault it was that I was out there by the side of the road.

They get along fine except when it's about me.

I make them fight.

"You better go home," I said. "I'm gonna spend the night by the side of the road."

That ended the fight.

My mother pleaded with me, then she cried.
I felt for her, but they're the ones who started this.

Not her exactly, but she married him. And if he thought it helped hearing him
mutter into the dashboard, "Crazy kid, makes me sick . . ."

All it helped was for me to make up my mind that I was gonna stay
by the side of the road that night. And the next night. And the next.

And the next. And the next. And the next.
The last thing I heard my mother say when they drove off was
"He'll need a sleeping bag and a pillow."

The last thing I heard my father say was
"That way he'll never learn his lesson!" It was a shout, really.

So . . .

I lived by the side of the road.

And you know, I got used to it. I even loved it. My mother brought me a poncho for when it rained. And a snowsuit for when it snowed.

The creek by the side of the road froze in winter.
My mother bought me ice skates.

In the summer, I swam in it. My brother Rudy was jealous,
so my mother let him swim in the creek with me.

And that caused trouble because then Rudy wanted to move in.

It was about then that my father talked me into letting him
build a little house for me out of aluminum siding.

Maybe because he was trying to make up to me,
he made it bigger than I needed. So I had plenty of room.

But I didn't let Rudy move in.
One of us had to stay home and grow up with them.

And since living by the side of the road was my idea,
why should my little brother get in on a good thing that wasn't even his idea—
and hurt my parents when they were already hurt enough.

They tried not to show that they were hurt, like this was some kind of phase I was going through and they were taking it in their stride.

They hired a tutor to give me lessons and homework.
I studied hard and got straight A's, not that I cared about the lessons, or thought they would do me much good. I did it to please my parents.

Sometimes you have to make concessions.

A thousand cars must have stopped to bother me.
The mothers and fathers in the cars called me names, like "Selfish."
The kids in them wanted to get out and come live with me.

I didn't ask for all this. So I dug a tunnel underneath the side of the road.

And I moved my little house inside the tunnel.

My father tried to help me, but I had my own ideas.

My father put in a small generator so I could have lights to read by.
My mother bought me a TV and, for Christmas, a computer.

I played games on the computer but didn't watch the TV—

except sometimes, like if I got sick. There were just too many things to do.

I dug extra tunnels and stuck my secret stuff in them.

Each tunnel had a different secret:

my comic-book superhero collection, thrillers, and a collection of
bottles thrown out of car windows. They were mostly beer,
but some were soda, some were wine.

Another collection of bubble wrap, and old magazines with articles
on sports and music and movies and serial killers.

A complete deck of cards, but every card came from a different deck,
a colored-rubber-band collection, a bottle-tops-from-all-nations collection.
I was the only person who could decode which tunnel was which.

I went outside only when I had to, because my mother didn't like my color so she wanted me to get some air.

I played ball, bouncing it by the side of the road and catching it one-handed. The tunnel was too small for a good game of catch, even by myself.

I was getting famous.
Some kids liked to come and hang out and play ball with me

and show off that they were better than me as ballplayers,
which made them feel okay about not living in a tunnel.

You wouldn't believe how many kids were jealous of me.
Some even came by to beat me up, but the other kids chased them away.

The ones who didn't want to beat me up wanted to move in.

When I was seventeen, a girl came by to meet me.

I was getting a little tired of all these girls coming by just because I was older. But this one—Daisy—wasn't such a pest. I don't know why, she asked me the same question every other girl asked.

"Don't you get lonely living by yourself by the side of the road?"
Every time I heard that question, which was a lot, I thought: How stupid can you get?

But not when *she* asked it. For the first time the question made sense.
I felt sick with loneliness.

She had gray eyes, at least in the tunnel, and white skin that looked like
it didn't get outdoors any more than I did. Even if I was sick with loneliness,
I wasn't going to tell her. I said, "No, I don't get lonely, I never get lonely."

But Daisy knew I was lying.
The next day she moved into the tunnel to the left of mine.

I meant to kick her out.

She really knew how to fix up a tunnel. We started hanging with each other.

She moved in her computer. She e-mailed from her tunnel to mine.
I e-mailed her back. The things we said in e-mail we never said in person.

We got married in a couple of years.

Eventually we had to expand the tunnel to make room for children.

Daisy wanted to bring in an architect, and I said, "Not in my tunnel."
That was our first fight.

The person she found wasn't all that bad, and had some good ideas.
Some we even used.

My father drove by one day.

He said, "Your brother Rudy left us to go to college and join the Navy.
Your mother and I are all alone with no children to take care of."

So my father and mother built a tunnel next to ours. At first, I was worried about it, but actually they turned out to be a great help with our kids, Kevin and Mary Beth.

My brother Rudy, when he got out of the Navy, wanted to come live with us.

But there wasn't room for any more people in our tunnel.

So he went away mad, got rich, got married,
and built a bigger, more state-of-the-art tunnel in Seattle.

Our whole family visits his family every summer

and you should see us oooh and aaah over his advanced technology.
His tunnel is more like a palace. Or half palace, half laboratory.

Still, Mom and Dad and Daisy and the kids are glad when
the visit's run its course and we can head back to our side of the road.

One or another of us will spring the trapdoor leading down to our tunnel.

The minute the last of us is inside and the trapdoor is closed
and we're safe and snug—

We always say the same thing: